Fairytale things to make and do

Leonie Pratt

Designed and illustrated by
Josephine Thompson and Katie Lovell

Additional illustration by
Stella Baggott, Nelupa Hussain, Jan McCafferty,
Sam Meredith and Antonia Miller

Edited by Fiona Watt

Steps illustrated by Stella Baggott
Photographs by Howard Allman

Contents

Fairytale wall hanging

Cut the slits about a finger's width apart.

1. Cut out a paper rectangle for the quilt. Draw a line across the top, then cut lots of slits up into the paper, as far as the line.

2. Cut lots of strips from bright paper. The strips can be different widths, but they must be longer than the width of the quilt.

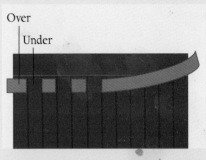

Over

Under

3. Weave a paper strip over and under the strips in the quilt, like this. Then, push the strip up so that it touches the pencil line.

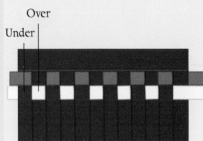

Over

Under

4. Weave a second strip so that it goes under, then over, the strips in the quilt. Then, push it up so that it touches the first one.

The tape secures the strips.

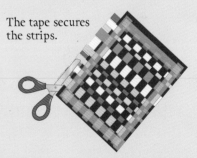

5. Weave more strips into the quilt in the same way. Turn the quilt over and tape along the edges. Then, cut the ends off the strips.

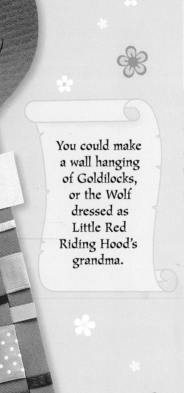

You could make a wall hanging of Goldilocks, or the Wolf dressed as Little Red Riding Hood's grandma.

Make the bed the same width as the quilt.

6. Cut out a bed from thick paper and glue the quilt onto it. Cut shapes for a pillow and the top of a sheet, then glue them on.

7. Cut shapes for the wolf's head and bonnet, then glue them together. Cut out eyes and ears and glue them on, then draw a face.

8. Glue the head onto the pillow. Cut out two paws, glue them on, then draw the claws. Tape a ribbon onto the back, for hanging.

This quilt has ribbon and patterned paper woven into it, too.

Tiaras for fairytale princesses

1. Cut a wide band of thin cardboard that fits around your head. Cut a little off one end, so that the tiara will sit on top of your head.

Roll the strip tightly.

2. For a rose, cut a strip of paper as wide as your finger and twice as long. Fold over a little at one end, then roll the strip to the other end.

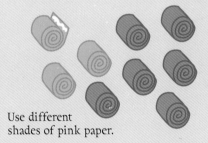

Use different shades of pink paper.

3. Let the strip unroll a little, then glue it to hold it together. Cut eight more strips from pink paper and make more roses.

Glue two roses above the others.

4. Pour white glue onto an old plate. Dip one side of a rose into the glue and press it onto the tiara. Glue on the other roses in a line.

5. Cut four more dark pink strips and four pale ones. Glue a dark strip onto one end of each pale strip. Then, roll them into big roses.

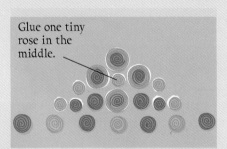

Glue one tiny rose in the middle.

6. Glue the big roses onto the tiara, like this. Then, cut seven very short strips and roll them into tiny roses. Glue them on, too.

Make glittery jewels like the ones above by following step 3 on page 17.

The top edges of these butterfly wings were dipped into white glue and then into glitter.

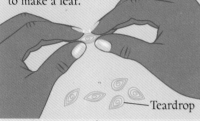

Pinch like this to make a leaf.

Teardrop

7. Make lots of small green rolls. Then, to make a teardrop, pinch one side of the roll. To make a leaf, pinch both sides.

You will need to clip the tiara into your hair with hair clips.

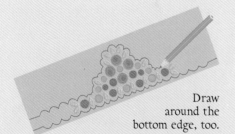

Draw around the bottom edge, too.

8. Glue the teardrops and leaves between the roses. Draw around the shapes, leaving a small border. Then, cut along the lines.

9. Cut halfway up into one end of the tiara. Then, cut halfway down into the other end. Slot the ends of the tiara together, like this.

Other ideas

For a butterfly wing, roll a long strip, then make two pinches on one side.

For a heart, make a large teardrop, then press into the round end with your fingernail.

Rapunzel in the tower

You only need one half for the roof.

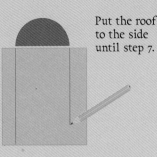

Put the roof to the side until step 7.

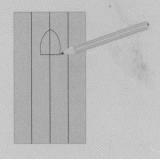

1. To make the roof, draw around a small plate on thick paper. Cut out the circle, fold it in half, then unfold it. Cut along the line.

2. Lay the roof at the top of a piece of thick paper. Draw lines down from each end. Then, cut along the lines to make the tower.

3. Draw a line down the middle of the tower. Then, add lines on either side of it, like this. Draw a window over the middle line, too.

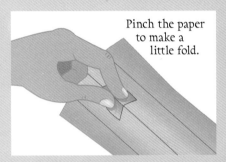

Pinch the paper to make a little fold.

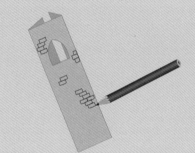

The front of the tower will curve as you overlap the edges.

4. Pinch the paper in the middle of the window. Make a cut into the fold, then cut out the window, starting from the cut.

5. Fold the edges back, along the lines on either side of the window. Erase the middle pencil line, then draw bricks on the tower.

6. To make the tower 3-D, turn it over and pull the edges together until they overlap. Then, use sticky tape to secure the edges.

Erase the middle line when the ink is dry.

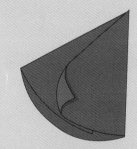

To make trees like these, follow step 2–3 on page 4 to make green and pink rolls, then glue the rolls onto a paper tree.

7. With a pencil, draw lines on the roof to divide it into four sections, like this. Use a felt-tip pen to draw tiles on the two middle sections.

8. Fold back the outer sections, along the pencil lines. Then, pull the edges together until they overlap, and secure them with tape.

The windowsill should be wider than the window.

9. Draw Rapunzel's head and long hair on a piece of paper. Add the top of her body and a windowsill. Then, fill her in using pencils.

10. Cut out Rapunzel. Glue the windowsill below the window. Then, spread white glue around the top of the tower and push the roof on.

In the fairytale, Rapunzel was trapped in a tower and the only way anyone could reach her was by climbing up her long hair.

You could glue your tower onto a paper background, like this one.

Prince to the rescue!

1. Pour some thick white paint onto an old plate. Dip your finger into the paint, then finger paint a long oval for the horse's body.

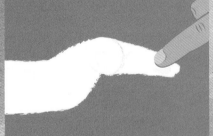

2. Finger paint a thick curve for the neck. Then, add a shape for the horse's head, so that it overlaps the top of the neck.

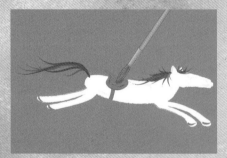

3. Finger paint the legs, then use a paintbrush to add the ears. Paint a mane and tail, hooves and a saddle with brown paint.

This horse had spots painted on the body in step 3.

To make a background like this one, brush watery paint over the paper. When the paint is dry, use chalks to draw swirls for the clouds.

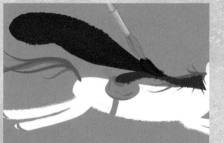

Use the gold pen to draw reins and stirrups, too.

4. When the paint is dry, paint a shape for the prince's body and arm above the horse's back. Add a long, flowing cloak, too.

5. Paint the prince's head, hand, leg and boot. Add his hair and beard. Then, paint a gold crown and add dots for eyes. Let the paint dry.

6. Use a black pen to draw a face on the prince and on the horse. Then, use a gold pen and glitter glue to decorate the prince's outfit.

Fairytale castle

Leave a space between the two towers.

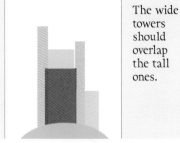

The wide towers should overlap the tall ones.

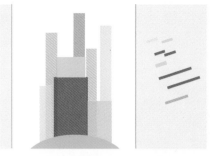

1. Cut out a hill and two tall, thin towers from tissue paper. Glue the hill onto a piece of thick white paper, then glue on the towers.

2. Cut out a bright pink tower and glue it on. Cut two short, wide towers, too. Glue one above the pink tower, and one next to it.

3. Cut three thin towers from blue and lilac tissue paper. Glue them on. Then, cut lots of very thin strips from tissue paper.

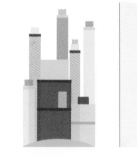

4. Trim the thin strips to fit across the towers, then glue them on. Then, cut seven small rectangles and glue them on, like this.

5. Cut out pointed roofs and glue them on. Cut out flags, too. Glue them on, leaving a space for a flagpole between the flag and the roof.

6. Cut out a door and glue it onto the bright pink tower. Add a round window, then cut shapes for bushes and glue them onto the hill.

Glue the long strips on first.

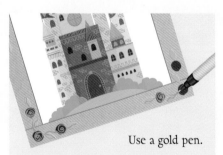

Use a gold pen.

7. Draw lots of windows using felt-tip pens. Then, use a gold pen to draw details on the castle such as flagpoles and battlements.

8. For the frame, cut four paper strips, making two as tall as the paper, and two as wide. Glue them around the edges of the paper, like this.

9. Cut circles for roses from tissue paper and glue them onto the frame. Glue on leaves, then draw spirals on the roses, and add stems.

Little Red Riding Hood

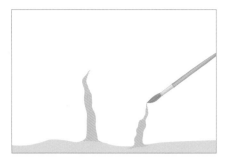

1. Brush watery green paint over the bottom of a piece of paper, for the grass. Then, paint some pale purple tree trunks.

2. Paint branches on the pale purple trunks. Then, paint some darker purple trees in the same way. The trees should overlap a little.

3. Paint black trees over the purple ones. Then, add a big black tree coming in from the edge of the paper. Leave the paint to dry.

4. Draw a circle for Red Riding Hood's head, below the branches of a tree. Use a black pencil to draw her hair, then add her face.

5. Draw a hood and cloak, then add her hands and a basket. Draw frills for the dress and add legs. Fill her in using watery paints.

6. Cut out lots of little leaves from paper from old magazines. Glue them onto the branches, gluing darker leaves onto the black trees.

7. Cut out shapes for apples and flowers from old magazine paper. Glue them on, then use a pencil to draw their stems and leaves.

This wolf was drawn with a black pencil, then filled in with watery paints.

Frog Prince

1. Cut a piece of foil as big as this page. Gently scrunch it into an egg shape. Then, flatten the small end for the frog's mouth.

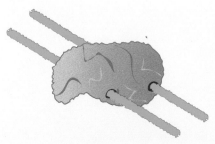

2. Carefully push a pencil through the foil to make two holes where the legs will go. Push a green pipe cleaner through each hole.

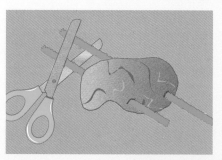

3. Squeeze the foil tightly to make it firm, especially where the legs join the body. Then, cut a little piece off each of the front legs.

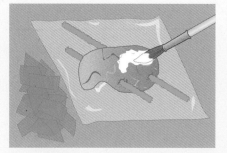

4. Cut lots of pieces of green tissue paper. Then, lay the frog on a piece of plastic foodwrap and brush part of it with white glue.

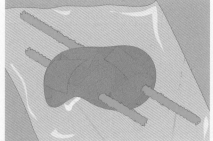

5. Press pieces of tissue paper onto the wet glue. Brush on more glue and press on more tissue paper, until the frog is covered.

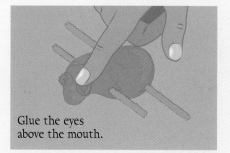

Glue the eyes above the mouth.

6. Cut two pieces of tissue paper as big as the body. Dip them in glue and roll them into two balls. Glue on the balls, for eyes.

In 'The Frog Prince', the princess kisses a frog and it turns into a prince.

The frog should sit upright.

7. When the glue is dry, use a small paintbrush to paint the frog's eyes. Then, draw a wide smile with a black felt-tip pen.

8. Cut four short pieces of pipe cleaner. Then, twist one piece around each leg. Do this a little way from the end, like this.

9. Bend the back legs up, then down, to make 'knees'. Bend the front legs to make 'elbows' and bend the feet so that they point forward.

You could make a Frog Princess as well, like this one.

10. Glue shiny paper or foil onto thick paper. Draw a small crown and cut it out. Fold the bottom back and glue it onto the frog's head.

The Princess and the pea

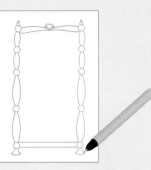

1. Use a pencil to draw a tall bed frame, like this. Add a heart at the top. Then, go over the pencil lines and fill in the frame with a gold pen.

Glue the mattresses so that they overlap.

2. Cut out a mattress and a pea from paper. Glue them onto the bed. Then, cut more mattresses from patterned paper and glue them on, too.

3. Cut out a blanket, sheet and pillows and glue them on. Cut out the princess's head, hair and hand, and glue them on. Draw a face.

In the fairytale, the princess can't sleep because she can feel a pea through the pile of mattresses.

Cinderella's sparkly slipper

1. Draw a shape for a slipper on a piece of thin white cardboard. Then, cut it out and lay it on a piece of newspaper.

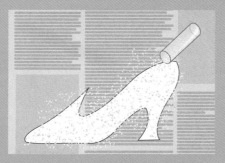

2. Brush white glue all over the slipper and sprinkle glitter over it. Let the glue dry, then shake off any excess glitter.

3. For the jewels, cut two small pieces of tissue paper. Spread glue on your fingers and roll each piece into a ball. Roll them in glitter.

4. Dab glue onto the jewels and press them onto the slipper. Then, glue sequins and tiny beads onto the slipper, to decorate it.

Make the cushion a little longer than the slipper.

5. Cut a cushion from paper and draw gold lines across it. Then, cut two tassels from gold paper and glue them on. Glue the slipper on top.

Cinderella lost one of her glass slippers when she ran from the ball at midnight.

Gingerbread house collage

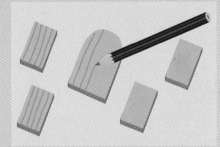

Paint the frames on top of the windows.

1. Paint a hill with a brown house on top. Cut windows from shiny paper and glue them on. Then, paint the frames using thick paint.

Glue the shutters beside the windows.

2. Cut out a door and four shutters from an old cardboard box. Paint them, then use a pencil to drag lines in the wet paint.

3. Cut strips from the box for the roof and top of the chimney, then paint them. When the paint is dry, glue everything onto the house.

You could use shiny paper or cellophane, too.

Paint the circles really thickly.

4. For a wrapped chocolate, cut a small square of foil. Roll a ball of tissue paper and put it on the non-shiny side of the foil.

5. Fold in two edges of the foil so that they overlap. Then, twist the foil on either side of the ball. Make more chocolates in this way.

6. For chocolate drops, mix white paint with a little yellow or pink. Mix in some white glue, then paint lots of circles on thick paper.

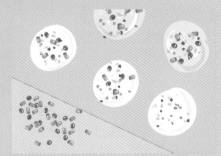

Sprinkle glitter over the swirls and strawberries.

7. While the paint is still wet, sprinkle glitter and tiny beads onto the circles. Cut out the chocolate drops when the paint is dry.

8. Mix paint and white glue, then paint candy canes, strawberries, chocolate swirls and lollipops. When they are dry, cut them out.

9. Glue chocolates onto the roof and above the door. Then, glue strawberries onto the shutters. Glue the canes and lollipops onto the hill.

Hansel and Gretel were very excited when they saw the gingerbread house. They didn't know that a witch lived inside.

This path was cut from paper, then decorated with circles cut from shiny paper.

These lollipops have toothpicks for sticks.

Trolls and ogres

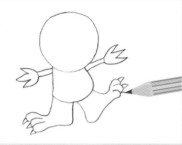

1. Draw a circle for a troll's head. Then, draw the body, with a rounded tummy. Draw the arms and legs, adding claws on the feet.

You could paint a scene of trolls and ogres playing hide-and-seek among the trees.

1...2...3...4...

2. Draw some spiky hair on top of the head and add two ears. Then, erase the pencil lines that overlap the hair and top of the ears.

Erase these lines.

3. Draw the eyes and a long nose. Add a mouth with a sharp tooth and draw the clothes. Then, erase any overlapping pencil lines.

4. Use runny orange paint to fill in the troll's head, hands and feet. Then, use bright shades of runny paint to fill in his clothes.

5. For an ogre, draw a big shape like a potato. Draw the arms, then add two rectangles for legs. Draw a boot at the end of each leg.

Draw the legs of a troll hiding in a tree.

You could draw a troll's head peeking out from the top of a tree.

6. Draw a curve for the ogre's chin. Then, draw the face, with a round nose and big teeth. Add ears, horns and wispy hair.

This part was erased.

7. Draw a curve under each arm, then add a belt. Erase part of the line across the left leg. Then, draw stripes below the belt, like this.

8. Use runny purple paint to fill in the ogre's head and arms. Then, use different shades of bright paint to fill in the rest of him.

You could put
any picture in
your frame.

In the story 'Snow White',
the wicked queen asks:

"Mirror, mirror on the wall,
Who is the fairest of
them all?"

She is very upset when
the mirror shows an
image of Snow White.

Snow White picture frames

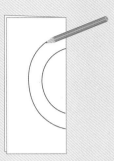

1. Fold a piece of thin cardboard in half. Then, draw two curves against the fold. Make one curve larger than the other.

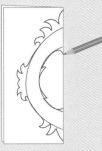

2. Draw lots of fancy shapes on the outside curve, like this. Then, draw some shapes on the inside of the frame, too.

3. Keeping the cardboard folded, cut around the outside of the frame. Then, cut out the middle. Open the frame and lay it flat.

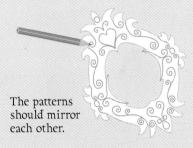

The patterns should mirror each other.

4. Draw a heart at the top of the frame. Draw swirly patterns on one side of the frame, then draw the same patterns on the other side.

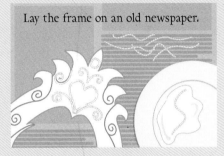

Lay the frame on an old newspaper.

5. Cut pieces of string that are the same length as the patterns. Dip them in white glue, then press them over the patterns on the frame.

Press the paper into the patterns with a paintbrush.

6. Rip tissue paper into pieces. Brush glue over the string and frame, then press on the paper, folding it over the edges. Leave it to dry.

Use gold paint, if you have some.

7. Dip the tip of a dry paintbrush into some paint and brush it gently over the frame. Then, paint along the string patterns. Let it dry.

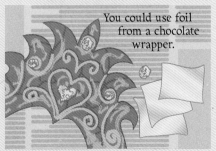

You could use foil from a chocolate wrapper.

8. For the jewels, cut four pieces of foil, then roll each one into a small ball. Glue the jewels inside the shapes on the frame.

9. Lay the frame on a picture. Turn both of them over and tape the picture in place. Then, tape on a piece of ribbon, for hanging.

Puss in Boots puppets

Draw the head near the top of the paper.

Draw the belt halfway up the body.

1. Draw a shape for a cat's head on a piece of paper. Draw a curved line for the brim of the hat, then draw ears and the top of the hat.

2. Draw the face, then the body and 'arms'. Draw a tail and add a belt across the tummy. Fill everything in using felt-tip pens.

Don't glue this part.

3. Cut around the outline. Then, fold up the bottom of the body, across the belt. Glue the rest of the body onto thin red cardboard.

4. Fold down the bottom of the body and draw a shape around it for the cloak. Cut along the cloak and around the top of Puss in Boots.

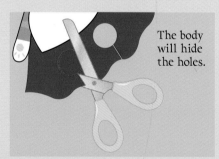

The body will hide the holes.

5. Fold up the body again. Draw two circles on the cloak, where your fingers will go. Cut up into the circles and cut around them.

6. Fold a piece of brown paper in half. Draw a boot against the fold, making the leg part as wide as two of your fingers.

This Puss in Boots puppet has a feather taped onto the back of the hat.

You could make high-heeled boots for the king's daughter.

24

In the fairytale, Puss in Boots tricks an ogre into giving him his castle. The king then believes that Puss's master is a rich man, so lets him marry his daughter.

Try making the ogre with big furry feet.

This puppet of Puss's master had the tops of the boots folded down before they were glued.

Push your fingers through the holes, then push the boots on, so that your knuckles are the 'knees'.

The toes of the boots should point different ways.

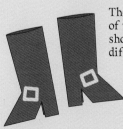

7. Draw a tab on the side of the boot. Then, keeping the paper folded, cut out the boot. Unfold it and cut off one of the tabs.

8. Draw around the shape on another piece of brown paper and cut out the shape. Fold over the tabs on both pairs of boots.

9. Spread glue on the tabs. Fold the boots in half and press hard. Turn one boot over, then draw a buckle on each boot with a gold pen.

Cinderella and her ugly sisters

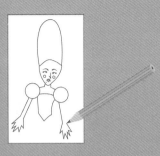

Glue a bead onto her hand for a ring.

1. Draw an ugly sister's head on thin cardboard. Add a face and a tall shape for the hair. Then, draw the body and arms and cut her out.

2. Draw over the pencil lines and fill her in using bright felt-tip pens. Then, glue beads around her neck, for a necklace.

3. Rip a cotton ball into small pieces and roll the pieces into balls. Spread white glue over the sister's hair and press on the balls.

You could use stickers from the middle of this book to decorate an ugly sister.

This ugly sister had spots and hearts cut from paper and glued onto her skirt.

Trim the ends along the bottom of the card.

Cinderella's old clothes were transformed by her Fairy Godmother into a beautiful gown so that she could go to a ball at the palace.

4. For the skirt, fold a piece of thin cardboard in half. Cut strips of paper or gift ribbon and glue them on. Then, trim the ends.

5. With the fold at the top, draw curves around the top corners of the card. Then, keeping the card folded, cut along the curves.

You could also make Cinderella in the same way.

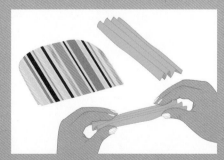

6. Cut two wide strips of tissue paper, a little longer than the skirt. Make lots of folds across the strips, to make them pleated.

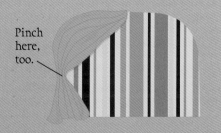

Pinch here, too.

7. Spread glue from the middle of the fold along one side of the skirt. Pinch the end of a strip and glue it around the skirt, like this.

Glue bows onto her skirt.

8. Glue the second strip on the other side of the skirt. Glue on the body. Then, cut paper bows and glue them onto her hair and dress.

Fairytale wedding

Use a pencil.

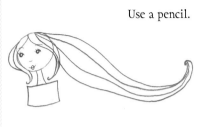

1. Draw a circle for the princess's head. Then, draw a neck and bodice. Draw her face, then add long wavy lines for the hair.

2. Draw a crown, then draw a long, flowing veil around the hair. Draw two circles, for shoulders, either side of the bodice.

3. Draw two sleeves with a hand at the end of each one. Draw the rest of the dress so that the hem curves up to one hand, like this.

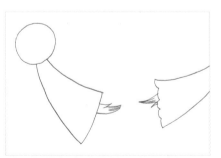

4. Draw a circle for the top of the prince's sleeve. Then, draw the rest of his arm reaching out for the princess. Add a hand, too.

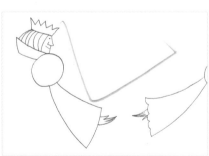

5. Draw the collar at the top of the sleeve. Draw a face and a crown. Then, add curved lines for hair, below the crown.

Paint blobs of watery
paint for the crowd,
then add outlines
and details with
black and gold pens.

Sleeping Beauty
marries the prince
who wakes her from
her sleep with a kiss.

The lines
are shown
in yellow
so that
you can
see them.

Use a gold
pen to fill
in both
crowns.

6. Draw a cloak curving
down to the ground, and
add two shoes at the
bottom. Then, draw the
prince's other arm.

7. Draw lines on the prince
and princess with wax
crayons. Use a white wax
crayon for the princess. Fill
them in with watery paints.

8. When the paint is dry,
use a thin black felt-tip pen
to draw over all the pencil
lines. Then, use a gold pen
to decorate their clothes.

Magic fairytale wands

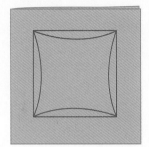

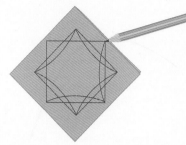

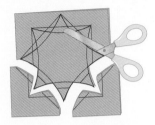

1. Fold a piece of thin cardboard in half and draw a square on it. Then, add curves inside the edges of the square.

2. Turn the cardboard a little. Then, draw another square over the first one, like this. Add curves inside the second square, too.

3. To make a star, draw around the outline of the curves with a red pencil. Cut out the star, through both layers of cardboard.

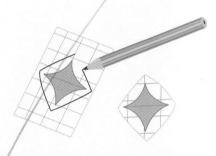

4. Hold the stars together and fold them in half. Draw a curved triangle against the fold and cut it out. Unfold all the shapes.

5. Lay the pieces from the middle of the stars onto some book covering film. Draw around them, leaving a border, then cut them out.

These wands had different shapes drawn in their middles in step 4.

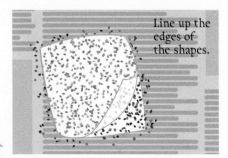

Line up the edges of the shapes.

6. Peel the backing paper off one shape and sprinkle a little glitter over it. Then, peel the paper off the other shape and press it on top.

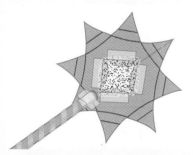

Hold the ribbon tightly as you tape it.

You could decorate your wand with stickers from the middle of this book.

7. Tape a long piece of gift ribbon onto one end of a straw. Wrap the ribbon around and around, then secure the end with tape.

8. Tape the straw onto the star that has pencil lines on one side of it. Then, tape the sparkly shape over the hole in the star.

Glue sequins on both sides.

9. Tie a piece of gift ribbon onto the straw, below the star. Then, glue the second star on top and decorate the wand with sequins.

Happily ever after...

The paints will bleed into each other.

Leave space for a window.

1. Brush watery yellow paint across the top of a piece of paper. Brush orange, then red, down to the bottom of the paper. Let the paint dry.

2. Paint a road with thick black paint. Paint trees on either side of the road. Then, paint a big pumpkin shape for the carriage.

3. Draw swirls and wheels below the carriage, using a black pen. Draw a prince and princess in the window, then add details with a silver pen.

Photographic manipulation: John Russell and Nick Wakeford

First published in 2006 by Usborne Publishing Ltd., Usborne House, 83-85 Saffron Hill, London, England. www.usborne.com